T5-AQQ-646

JOE DiMAGGIO

by
William R. Sanford
&
Carl R. Green

CRESTWOOD HOUSE

New York

Maxwell Macmillan Canada
Toronto

Maxwell Macmillan International
New York Oxford Singapore Sydney

Library of Congress Cataloging-in-Publication Data
Sanford, William R. (William Reynolds), 1927–
    Joe DiMaggio / by William R. Sanford and Carl R. Green. — 1st ed.
       p. cm. — (Sports immortals)
    Includes bibliographical references and index.
    Summary: A biography of one of baseball's greatest players. Includes a trivia quiz.
    ISBN 0-89686-738-2
       1. DiMaggio, Joe, 1914– —Juvenile literature. 2. Baseball players—United States—Biography—Juvenile literature. 3.
    New York Yankees (Baseball team)—Juvenile literature. [1. DiMaggio, Joe, 1914– . 2. Baseball players.] I. Green, Carl R.
    II. Title. III. Series.
    GV865.D5S25   1993
    796.357'092—dc20
    [B]   91-42180

Photo Credits
All photos courtesy of The Bettmann Archive

Copyright © 1993 by Crestwood House, Macmillan Publishing Company

All rights reserved. No part of this book may be reproduced or transmitted in any form or by any means, electronic or
mechanical, including photocopying, recording, or by any information storage and retrieval system, without permission in
writing from the Publisher.

Macmillan Publishing Company   Maxwell Macmillan Canada, Inc.
866 Third Avenue   1200 Eglinton Avenue East
New York, NY 10022   Suite 200
                                      Don Mills, Ontario M3C 3N1

CRESTWOOD HOUSE

Macmillan Publishing Company is part of the Maxwell Communication Group of Companies.

Produced by Flying Fish Studio

Printed in the United States of America

First edition

10 9 8 7 6 5 4 3 2 1

CONTENTS

A ROOKIE LIGHTS UP NEW YORK

Good news was hard to find in the spring of 1936. Adolf Hitler was building a mighty war machine in Germany. A bloody civil war was brewing in Spain. In the United States, millions of workers had worries of their own. Jobs and money were scarce. The **Great Depression** held the nation in an iron grip.

In that season of despair, fans of the New York Yankees had reason to cheer. A **rookie** outfielder arrived to set the city on fire with his hitting and fielding. Although he was only 21, writers compared Joe DiMaggio to the great Babe Ruth.

George Moriarty, an American League umpire, praised the rookie. "Joe DiMaggio is the [best] ballplayer I have seen come up in the last 30 years," he said. "He is great now. He will be more amazing next season. . . . DiMaggio has power, and something extra. . . . He makes [tough] catches look simple because when the ball comes down, he has arrived. . . . He has no weaknesses."

Joe's fans held their breath when he was injured during **spring training**. At last, on May 3, he played his first game. In a 14–5 win over the St. Louis Browns, he smashed a triple and two singles. Five days later, against Detroit, he threw a runner out at the plate. The bull's-eye throw saved the game for New York.

Some rookies fade after a hot start, but Joe was just getting warmed up. On Memorial Day, he singled to tie the game in the 9th. Then he won it with a triple in the 12th. As late as June 24, his **batting average** was a sparkling .360. That was the day Joe tied a **major league** record by hitting two home runs in the same inning. For the season, he hit .323, batted in 125 runs, and hit 29 home runs. In the World Series, his nine hits helped the Yankees crush the Giants in six games.

Joe McCarthy was the Yankee manager that year. Later, when asked about Joe's hitting, McCarthy said, "Well, he was just about the best. ... He didn't care who was pitching. ... And he could do it in the eighth and ninth innings when the game was on the line."

Plenty of young ballplayers have talent but never make it to the big leagues. What made Joe different? McCarthy explained, "Joe really studied the game. He thought about baseball all the time. ... He never made a mental mistake. He never missed a sign; he never threw the ball to the wrong base."

Baseball stars inspire nicknames and the rookie earned his share. Sportswriters called him Joltin' Joe and the Yankee Clipper. Back home in San Francisco, his parents were thrilled by their son's success. But they still called him Giuseppe.

TRIVIA 1*

When Joe broke in as a rookie in 1936, he relaxed at night by reading and listening to the radio. What reading materials and radio shows did he favor?

* Answers to all Trivia Quiz questions can be found on page 47.

GROWING UP IN SAN FRANCISCO

Joe DiMaggio never played catch with his father. Giuseppe Paolo DiMaggio was too busy making a living. He was an immigrant who left his native Sicily in 1902 to settle in California. Like most new Americans, Giuseppe wanted a better life for himself and his family. The first work he found was on the railroad—for ten cents an hour. After months of hard labor, he was able to send for his wife, Rosalie.

Joe DiMaggio at the age of three standing outside his home in Martinez, California

7

The DiMaggio family grew quickly. The couple's eighth child was born on November 25, 1914, in Martinez, California. The baby was given the English form of his father's name—Joseph Paul DiMaggio. When Joe was a few months old, the family moved to San Francisco. In all, 11 DiMaggios lived in the four-room house on Taylor Street. In time, Giuseppe was able to buy his own fishing boat. Each morning he sailed the *Rosalie D.* out from Fisherman's Wharf to catch crabs and fish.

Even as a child, Joe knew he did not want to be a fisherman. He disliked the smell of fish, and the rocking of the boat made him seasick. He stayed in bed when the older boys left for the day's fishing. In the afternoons, he tried to make himself scarce when the boats returned. That sometimes saved him from cleaning fish, mending nets and scrubbing the boat. Giuseppe was certain his lazy son would grow up to be a bum.

Money was scarce in the DiMaggio household. Joe often wore hand-me-down clothes that his brothers had outgrown. By the time he was ten, he had discovered his great love—baseball. Rosalie scolded him for coming home with his pants ripped, but Joe just smiled. His speed, strength and quick hands made him a star in the local **sandlot games**.

Joe played on a field called the Horse Lot. To start a game, the boys had to shoo away the horses that were kept there. Then they marked the bases with rocks and mended torn baseballs with tape. A sawed-off oar served as a bat. Gloves were a luxury and most of the boys played bare-handed. When he was 13, Joe moved up to the Boys Club League. Playing with good equipment for the first time, he led the Jolly Knights to a championship.

Joe was always shy. At home he joined in the noisy family debates, but around strangers he kept quiet. After school he sold newspapers on a street corner. Unlike most newsboys, he did not yell, "Paper! Get your paper here!" Across the street his younger brother Dominic often outsold him.

For a while Joe tried tennis, but he liked team sports better. By then, his older brother Vince was making $25 a game as a **semipro** baseball player. School seemed pointless to a boy who wanted to be a professional baseball player. When Joe was 17, he dropped out of Galileo High School. He took a job in an orange juice plant and did odd jobs on the wharf.

Joe's baseball talent won him a place on the Rossi Olive Oil Company team. Again he led his team to a title, hitting two home runs in the championship game. In 1932, the same players moved up to the Sunset Produce League. Joe batted a sizzling .633 in 18 games. But Class B semipro ball was a long way from the major leagues. Joe set his sights on breaking in with the Class Triple A San Francisco Seals.

Joe was famous for using his speed to turn singles into doubles. Despite this, his best base-stealing year was 1938—when he stole only six bases. Why did he steal so seldom?

17-year-old Joe with the San Francisco Seals' manager, Ike Caveney

A ROOKIE TAKES THE COAST LEAGUE APART

Baseball talent ran deep among the DiMaggios. Tom, the oldest boy, turned down a chance to play for the Hollywood Stars. He loved the game, but the family needed him to help on the boat. In 1932, Vince signed with the San Francisco Seals. The Seals paid him $150 a month to play for their Tucson farm club.

Joe's fine play in the semipro leagues caught the eye of Pacific Coast League **scouts**. These hardheaded baseball men liked his speed, his strong wrists and his quiet confidence. Late in the summer of 1932, the San Francisco Missions offered him a contract. Joe held back. He wanted to talk it over with Vince, who had been called up to the Seals.

Spike Hennessy, a Seal scout, saw Joe peeking through a hole in the stadium fence. Spike had already scouted Joe and knew he had talent. He took the teenager to meet Charlie Graham, the club owner. Graham gave Joe a tryout at shortstop during the team's final three games. Joe passed the test with flying colors.

During spring training in 1933, the rookie won a place on the team with his bat. The manager moved him to the outfield after he saw Joe's problems at shortstop. As a right fielder, the 18-year-old soon mastered the art of catching fly balls. At home, Giuseppe no longer worried about his son's future. Joe's $250 monthly paycheck was big money during that depression year.

On his first day in the starting lineup, Joe cracked two base hits. That was only the start. From San Diego to Seattle, he rattled ballpark fences with scorching line drives. His 169 **RBIs** led the league. A .340 batting average and 28 homers put him among the league leaders. In the field, his strong arm kept base runners from taking extra bases. By midseason, major league scouts were keeping a close eye on the young star.

TRIVIA 3

During his 56-game hitting streak, Joe batted .408. Of his 91 hits, 15 were home runs and 4 were triples. How many runs did he score and how many of the hits were singles?

The scouts saw Joe shatter a league record set in 1914. From May 28 to July 25 he chalked up at least one hit in every game he played. A big crowd turned out to see him break the old record by hitting in game number 50. The mayor gave him a gold watch and his teammates added a check of their own. Joe then ran his string to 61 games before the streak ended.

At six feet one inch and 190 pounds, Joe impressed onlookers with his graceful play. In the clubhouse he was still shy and quiet. Because he seldom smiled, his teammates called him Poker Face. They forgot that Joe's parents spoke only Italian. He could not always keep up with their slangy, rapid English. Joe smiled even less after the Seals traded Vince to Hollywood.

If 1933 was a record year, 1934 was nearly a disaster. Joe was hitting .341 when he wrenched his knee climbing out of a cab. After sitting out for a week, he found that the knee buckled again when he tried to play. Doctors put his leg in a cast.

As a rule, scouts refused to take a chance on a player with a bad knee. Only Bill Essick, a New York Yankee scout, did not give up. On his advice, the Yankees bought Joe's contract for $25,000 and five players. The Seals insisted that their star be allowed to play one more year in the Coast League.

Joe used the extra year to prove that his knee was strong again. He hit an amazing .398, knocked in 154 runs and slammed 34 homers. The Yankees took one look at the numbers and told Joe to report to spring training in 1936.

TRIVIA 4

Sometimes players set personal records while their teams are doing poorly. What was the Yankee won-lost record during the 56 games of Joe's great hitting streak?

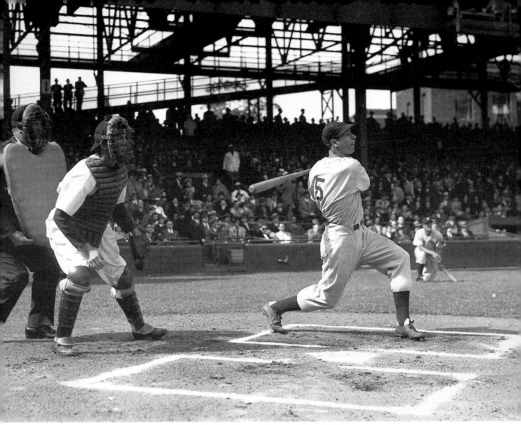

Joe cracks out a single for the Yankees during this 1936 game.

A YANKEE STAR IS BORN

The Yankees badly needed a new star. The once-mighty Bronx Bombers had not reached the World Series since 1932. Hungry for victories, fans hoped DiMaggio would bring new life to the team.

Yankee veterans Tony Lazzeri and Frankie Crosetti drove Joe to Florida that spring. During the long trip they gave Joe some advice. "Play hard and keep your mouth shut," they told him. When it was Joe's turn to drive, he admitted that he did not know how. "Let's throw the bum out," Lazzeri roared.

Spring training showed that Joe could hit major league pitching. A New York writer reported, "Joe [is] living up to all the advance notices. ... He [slashes] sharp hits to all corners of the Florida ballparks." Then Joe was struck by the spring injury jinx that always seemed to haunt him. After he sprained an ankle, a trainer burned his foot during a heat treatment.

After Joe's foot healed, Manager Joe McCarthy played him in left field. Center field was Joe's natural position, but Ben Chapman was a fixture there. The Yankees traded Chapman later that season to clear the way for their prize rookie. McCarthy did not try to change Joe's flawless batting style. His powerful, level swing met the ball squarely no matter where it was pitched. Pitchers sometimes fooled him, but not for long.

The rookie helped the Yankees win the American League **pennant** with a .323 batting average. Then he improved to .346 in the World Series win over the Giants. The Yankees rewarded him with a raise to $15,000. That winter, Joe bought his parents a new house.

After being out for two weeks with bad tonsils, Joe started the 1937 season with a hot bat. Pitchers shook their heads and despaired of getting him out. Joltin' Joe led the league with 46 homers and drove in 167 runs. His batting average was a classy .346. Once again he led the Yankees to a World Series win.

When contract talks opened, the team offered $25,000. Joe said he wanted $40,000. This time Colonel Ruppert, the Yankee's owner, refused to budge. Joe held out during the spring but finally gave in. When he played his first game of 1938, the fans booed. People who were struggling through hard times did not feel sorry for a rich young ballplayer. The abuse lasted until July, when the

14

pennant race heated up. Joe's hitting and outfield play helped win a third straight pennant and World Series.

Joe went to spring training in 1939 and promptly tore the muscles above his ankle. Once again he missed some early season games. In August his bat came to life—in one 12-game stretch he batted a sizzling .509. Yankee fans also marveled at his catch of a Hank Greenberg fly ball. Joe caught the hard-hit ball over his shoulder on a dead run, 450 feet from home plate. Inspired by his play, the Yankees won the pennant and the World Series.

Everything Joe touched seemed to turn to gold. He opened a restaurant on Fisherman's Wharf that was a great success. After the season he married a pretty actress named Dorothy Arnold. The streets outside the church were packed with fans on the day of the wedding. Police had to clear a path for the wedding party.

Marriage did not end the injury jinx. A wrenched knee put Joe on the bench for three weeks in the spring of 1940. While he was gone the team fell into the cellar. Joe caught fire in July and won the batting crown with a .352 average. Even so, for the first time in five years the Yankees did not win the pennant.

Joe DiMaggio with his bride, Dorothy Arnold

15

THE YEAR OF THE STREAK

Americans were ready to relax during the summer of 1941. The Great Depression was ending and people had jobs again. In that happier mood, newspaper readers turned to the sports pages. Page one was full of stories about the war in Europe.

For boxing fans, there were stories about heavyweight champion Joe Louis. Racing fans thrilled to the great Whirlaway's Triple Crown victory. In Boston, a peerless hitter named Ted Williams was flirting with a .400 batting average. And in New York, Joe DiMaggio was making headlines again.

Early in the season, Joe had fallen into a long batting **slump**. Worried fans wondered if the 26-year-old star was slipping. Then, on May 15, Joe began to hit again. No one paid much attention at first. Then people recalled his 61-game streak in the Pacific Coast League. Joltin' Joe had something going!

Joe is safe at home as he scores another run for the Yankees.

By June, Joe was closing in on the Yankee record of 29 games. Roger Peckinpaugh, who shared the old mark, was in the stands on June 17. Joe cracked a single to set a new record of 30. Inspired by the streak, the Yankees moved into first place a week later.

As the streak went on, the pressure grew. Pitchers seldom gave Joe a good pitch to hit. No one wanted to give up a record-breaking hit. When Joe went out on the streets, fans tore at his clothing, hoping for a souvenir. Dozens of kids gathered outside his hotel to ask for autographs. Joe said later, "I got to know more back exits from hotels than any man in the world."

Now Joe was close to two all-time records. George Sisler had set the American League record of 41 in 1922. Wee Willie Keeler's major league record of 44 dated back to 1897. Base hits had come more easily in Keeler's day—foul balls did not count as strikes. Despite the growing pressure, Sisler's record fell on June 29. Fans were thrilled to learn that Joe had dedicated the hit to a dying boy.

A huge crowd packed Yankee Stadium on July 1. Could Joe tie the all-time record? The Yankee Clipper was up to the task. He hit safely in both games of a doubleheader to tie the record. On July 2 he broke Keeler's mark with a long home run.

Game after game, Joe added to his new record. At times he waited until his final at-bat before he hit safely. But all of his hits came on full swings. Perhaps he was tempted, but he never tried to bunt for a base hit.

The great streak ended at 56 on July 17. Twice Joe hit the ball hard, but Cleveland third baseman Ken Keltner snagged both ground balls. In the eighth inning, Joe bounced into a double play. As abruptly as it had started, the streak was over.

Joe began a new 16-game streak the next day. The one hitless game had cost him a big payday, he moaned. If he had reached 57, Heinz 57 foods would have paid him $10,000 for his endorsement.

Even without the streak, 1941 would have been a great year. Joe batted .357 and batted in 125 runs. The Yankees won the pennant and the World Series. After winning the league's Most Valuable Player award, Joe was named the U.S. Athlete of the Year. In October, Dorothy added to Joe's joy by giving birth to Joseph Paul DiMaggio, Jr.

Two months later, on December 7, the Japanese attacked Pearl Harbor. The United States was at war again.

You're never too young to learn! Joe is shown here tutoring his infant son in the art of batting.

JOE CHANGES UNIFORMS

Baseball was shaken by the war. President Franklin Roosevelt asked the teams to keep playing, but nothing seemed the same. Some well-known players joined the armed forces and others were **drafted**. Older players and untried rookies filled out the rosters. Crowds were smaller too. Fans thought twice before they used their gas ration to drive to a baseball game.

Joe did not expect to be called to military service. He was in his late 20s, married and the father of a child. His draft board put him in Class 3, to be drafted only in an emergency. Joe was also suffering from stomach ulcers. Many men with ulcers were classed as unfit for service.

The Yankees used the war as an excuse for asking players to take pay cuts. Joe pointed to the awards he won in 1941 and at last won a small raise. When the games started, angry fans yelled at the players. "If you can play ball," they jeered, "why aren't you in the service?"

Despite the taunts the Yankees won the pennant by nine games. Joe's average fell to .305, but he batted in 114 runs. As usual, New York was favored to win the World Series. The St. Louis Cardinals lost the opener but roared back to win four straight. It was the first Yankee loss in a World Series since 1926.

TRIVIA 5

The 56-game hitting streak helped Joe win the American League's Most Valuable Player award in 1941. Why did some fans claim that Ted Williams deserved to be named the MVP?

Little Joe snaps a photo of his famous daddy, Air Force Staff Sergeant, Joe DiMaggio.

Joe's home life was also in turmoil. Dorothy had moved to Reno, Nevada, to file for divorce. Joe loved her and the baby deeply, but baseball was his whole life. Dorothy often felt shut out. In December, Joe talked her into delaying the divorce. A month later he announced that he was going to enlist.

When Joe became an Army Air Force private, his salary dropped from $43,750 to $600 a year. Like many sports and film stars, he was given special duty. The air force sent him to Santa Ana Army Air Field in California. After being assigned to Special Services, Joe joined the camp's baseball team. The all-star center fielder was kept busy chasing base hits given up by **amateur** pitchers.

Joe's ulcers still bothered him. A big shock came when he learned that Dorothy was going through with the divorce. The decree was granted early in 1944. Joe hoped to win her back, but Dorothy married another man in 1946.

In 1944 Joe was promoted to staff sergeant. The air force sent him to Hawaii, where he played for the 7th Army Air Force team. For a while he led the league with a .441 batting average. In August the ulcers flared up and put him in the hospital. Joe refused to ask for a discharge. He did not want his fans to think he had quit while the war was still going on.

A job as a PE instructor in New Jersey came next. Joe was kept on a soft diet because of his ulcers, and his weight dropped from 210 to 187. He was still in New Jersey when the war ended in August 1945. A month later he was given his discharge.

Joe celebrated by taking Dorothy and Joe Junior to a double-header at Yankee Stadium. Then he returned to San Francisco to see the rest of his family. Larry MacPhail, the new president of the Yankees, called to say that the team wanted him back. The Yankee Clipper was still one of the biggest names in baseball. Joe was happy to sign a contract for his prewar salary. He owed Uncle Sam three years in back taxes.

JOE'S RETURN TO BASEBALL

With the war over, Joe turned to the challenge of a new baseball season. He knew that the war had stolen three of his best years. To get his 31-year-old body in shape, he worked out at the New York Athletic Club. Along with tough daily workouts, he also had to bear the burden of fame.

Pitcher Eddie Lopat described Joe's problem. "I think DiMaggio was the loneliest man I ever knew," Lopat said. "He couldn't even eat a meal in a hotel restaurant. The fans just wouldn't let him [alone]. He led the league in room service."

Joltin' Joe surrounded by autograph-seeking fans

Joe at bat in his first appearance for the Yankees since the end of World War II

After a good spring, Joe began the season with a bang. He slammed out 20 home runs in the first 41 games. Then the injury jinx caught up with him. In July he hurt his leg sliding into second base. The bad leg forced him to miss the All-Star Game. Joe felt better when his brother Dominic was picked to replace him in center field. Dom was having a fine year with the Boston Red Sox.

Joe's batting eye was off when he returned. Worse yet, his left foot was hurting. By season's end his average had fallen under .300 for the first time. But Joe was not the only Yankee who had a subpar year. The team finished 17 games behind Boston.

TRIVIA 6

Vince, Dom and Joe DiMaggio all played in the major leagues. Along with being outfielders, what else do the three brothers have in common?

Joe went under the knife to have a bone spur removed. The slow-healing incision kept him out of the lineup until late April. Thanks to hours of batting practice, he was soon swinging the bat like the Clipper of old. Then his right elbow began to ache. Somehow, Joe hid the fact that his throwing arm was hurting. When a game was on the line, he could still fire the ball to the plate.

Led by Joe's clutch hitting, the Yankees rallied to win the 1947 pennant. In the World Series, his home runs helped beat Brooklyn in seven games. Sportswriters named him the American League's Most Valuable Player for the third time.

That winter a doctor removed bone chips from Joe's elbow. The Yankees gambled that he would recover and signed him to a $70,000 contract. The gamble paid off when Joe batted .320 and slugged 39 home runs in 1948. In the season's first game he also proved that his arm was fit. His bullet throw cut down a runner who tried to take an extra base. But Joe's fine play could not keep the Yankees from falling to third place.

That winter the Yankees hired Casey Stengel as manager. They also signed the Clipper to baseball's first $100,000 contract. But hopes that he would have an injury-free year in 1949 had to be shelved. Joe's foot was acting up again. A new bone spur caused a stabbing pain each time he dug in at the plate. On the field, Joe played as if he were not hurt. Off the field, he hauled himself up stairs one step at a time.

New York City proclaimed October 1 Joe DiMaggio Day. After receiving tributes and gifts, the Yankee Clipper thanked his cheering fans. He ended his short speech by saying, "And I want to thank the Good Lord for making me a Yankee." In Boston, Joe had to smile when the fans paid tribute to Dom. They chanted, "He's better than his brother Joe, Dominic DiMaggio."

Baseball brothers, Dom (left) and Joe (right)

Joe gives thanks to his admirers on Joe DiMaggio Day at Yankee Stadium.

Although Joe missed a number of games, he still managed to bat .346. Shortstop Phil Rizzuto and catcher Yogi Berra held the team together. The pennant race went down to the final day of the season. With pitcher Vic Raschi on the mound, the Yankees held on to beat the Red Sox 5–3. Coach Bill Dickey was so excited he jumped up from the bench—and knocked himself out on the **dugout** roof. After that great finish, the team trounced Brooklyn in five games. Once again, Joltin' Joe was on top of the baseball world.

JOE HANGS UP HIS GLOVE

As he grew older, Joe found it easier to talk to sportswriters. In the spring of 1950, he told them, "Something tells me this year that's coming up could be a big one." He knew that at age 35 he did not have many more years left. Over the winter Joe played golf, hunted and walked up to 20 miles a day. His mother cooked his favorite foods.

After reporting in top shape, Joe went right to work. The Yankees won their first game 15-10 after falling behind 9–0. Inspired by that comeback, they went on to win the pennant by three games. In the World Series, the Yankees took on the Philadelphia Phillies. The old pros shocked the young Whiz Kids, winning the series in four games.

Joe reached several milestones in 1950. On June 20 he smacked a single for hit number 2,000. Reaching that goal confirmed the Clipper's place as one of baseball's greatest hitters. He also smashed three home runs in a game for the third time. All three homers traveled over 400 feet. Casey Stengel, with his team beset by injuries, put Joe at first base for one game. Joe fielded well enough but the switch upset his hitting. Casey quickly returned him to the outfield.

Joe plays first base for the first and only time during this 1950 game.

After hitting .301 in 1950, Joe slipped to .263 in 1951. Injuries to his neck, shoulder and leg limited him to only 116 games. Despite Joe's slump, the Yankees won another pennant and another World Series. The series victory was the club's tenth in Joe's 13 seasons as a Yankee. Low average or not, the club quickly offered him a new $100,000 contract.

After the long season, Joe toured the Orient with an All-Star team. Baseball-mad Japanese fans shouted, "Banzai DiMaggio!" when he hit a long home run. At each stop, reporters asked him if he was going to retire. Each time, he put them off.

The Yankee Clipper hits a double during one of the last games of his major-league career.

Joe poses against a mural of Yankee Stadium as he announces his retirement from baseball in 1951.

On December 11, 1951, Joe held a press conference at the Yankee office in New York. "You all know I have had more than my share of physical injuries and setbacks during my career," he said. "In recent years these have been much too frequent to laugh off. When baseball is no longer fun, it's no longer a game. And so, I've played my last game of ball."

Joe spoke slowly and with emotion. "I feel that I have reached the stage where I can no longer produce for my ball club, my manager, my teammates and my fans."

Later, he added another reason for quitting. "I once made a promise to myself that I wouldn't try to hang on once the end was in sight," he explained. "I've seen too many beat-up players struggle to stay up there. It was always a sad sight."

TRIVIA 7

In a poll taken by the Associated Press, seven men were picked as the best players of baseball's first 50 years. Where did Joe rank in the list of seven? Who were the other six?

A reporter asked Casey Stengel who would take Joe's place. The manager said that no one could replace DiMaggio, "the greatest player I ever managed."

But ol' Casey had an ace up his sleeve. Mickey Mantle, a 19-year-old switch-hitter from Oklahoma, was ready and waiting. Just as Joe had replaced Babe Ruth, Mantle was about to become the next great Yankee outfielder. Neither Mantle nor anyone else would wear number 5, however. The Yankees retired Joe's number soon after he announced his retirement.

Baseball fans will remember Joe for awesome plays like this, where he steals third base in the ninth inning to win the game for the Yankees.

FALLING IN LOVE AGAIN

Joe's retirement opened a new chapter in his life. Money was no problem, for he had invested wisely. He slept late, played gin rummy with friends and went fishing. After he hit some poor golf shots, he took lessons. The Clipper wanted to do everything well.

When the baseball season opened, Joe began a television career. He was paid $50,000 to do interviews on the Yankees' pregame and postgame shows. Joe later became more polished, but in 1952 he was ill at ease before the camera. If someone mixed up his cue cards, he panicked.

With spring came a new romance. It all started when Joe saw pictures of Gus Zernial and a blond actress. Gus, a star with the Athletics, told Joe, "She was the most beautiful girl I had ever seen." He said her name was Marilyn Monroe.

Joe called Marilyn's agent and asked him to arrange a date. The agent set up a double date at a New York restaurant. As often happened, Marilyn was two hours late. She talked mostly about her movies and Joe, shy as always, said very little.

A day later, Joe phoned to ask for a second date. Marilyn said she was busy. After she turned him down every day for two weeks, he stopped calling. A week later, Marilyn phoned and said he could take her to dinner. After that, they saw each other often.

Vince, Dom and Joe combined to hit 573 home runs in their major league careers. That total is good for second place in the Brothers with Most Home Runs category. Which two brothers hold the all-time record?

Marilyn needed a strong man who could make her feel loved and safe. Most of the men she dated fell in love with her sexy public image. Joe, famous in his own right, loved her for herself.

After dating for over a year, Joe and Marilyn married in January 1954. They spent a quiet honeymoon in the mountains and then flew to Japan. Joe had promised to play in some exhibition games. Marilyn left him there to sing for U.S. troops in Korea. Joe did not say much, but he was upset. He wanted his bride to give up her career and become a housewife.

Marilyn was bubbling with pleasure when she returned from her tour. "Joe," she said, "you've never heard such cheering."

Quietly, Joe replied, "Yes, I have."

Joe fumed some more when Marilyn began work on *The Seven Year Itch*. The scene that upset him most showed Marilyn standing on a subway grating. A concealed wind machine blew her skirt above her waist. That was too much for the jealous husband. He flew back to San Francisco, leaving Marilyn to finish the film.

Soon the two were spending more and more time apart. Their arguments grew more fierce, for Marilyn refused to give up her career. In October, after only nine months of marriage, she filed for divorce. "If she wants the divorce, she will get it," Joe told a pack of reporters.

Despite the breakup, Joe and Marilyn were still friends. People close to Joe say he never stopped loving her. Marilyn later

TRIVIA 9

During his 13-year major league career, Joe seemed to be in every World Series and All-Star Game that came along. How many World Series and All-Star Games did he play in?

Film star Marilyn Monroe with baseball hero Joe DiMaggio on their wedding day

remarried, but Joe never did. A few years later, with her new marriage and career in tatters, Marilyn took her own life. Joe stepped in and arranged her funeral. He allowed only a handful of close friends to attend the service. Because he blamed the Hollywood crowd for her death, he refused to invite them.

A few years later, a magazine offered Joe $50,000 for a brief interview about Marilyn. He turned down the offer.

A LONG AND ACTIVE RETIREMENT

After Marilyn's death, Joe dropped out of the public eye for a few years. His fans were pleased to learn that he still sent roses to her grave each week. For his part, Joe was yearning to return to baseball—but not as a manager. He said he did not want to be in charge of 25 hard-to-handle ballplayers.

Former Yankee great Joe DiMaggio pays a charity visit to "Boy's Town" in Rome, Italy.

Joe singles to left field in the second inning of this 1968 Old Timers' game.

At last, in 1968, Joe found the right job. The Kansas City A's were moving to Oakland and wanted him to help build fan support. Joe became vice president and coach of the transplanted team. He helped sell the Oakland A's to Bay Area fans and worked with its young players. Reggie Jackson, one of the players he coached, became the team's star slugger. When the A's won their first pennant, Joe beamed with pride.

Joltin' Joe was a fixture at the yearly **old-timers games** in Yankee Stadium. His hair was graying but he was still slender and graceful. When he stepped on the field, the crowd cheered itself hoarse. As much as he enjoyed the games, Joe stopped playing when he reached his late 50s. He did not want fans to remember him as an inept old man.

The DiMaggio brothers are reunited at this 1986 Old Timers' game. Joe stands to the left, at age 72, next to Dom, 69, and Vince, 74.

Baseball observed its 100th birthday in 1969. The results of a national poll were announced at a grand banquet in Washington, D.C. Babe Ruth won the award as Greatest Player Ever. Then astronaut Frank Borman presented the Greatest Living Player award. To no one's surprise, the honor went to Joe DiMaggio.

Although he did not seek the spotlight, Joe had long been a household name. During his hitting streak in 1941, a hit song had swept the nation. Baseball fans hummed, "Joe . . . Joe . . . DiMaggio. . . .We want you on our side." Then, in the late 1960s, a Paul Simon song reached the top of the charts. "Mrs. Robinson" was a lament for a time when the world seemed simpler. "Where have you gone, Joe DiMaggio? A nation turns its lonely eyes to you," the first two lines pleaded.

Joe could only shake his head. "I never did understand that song," he said.

In the 1970s, the Clipper became a TV pitchman. In his sincere, low-key way, he talked about a coffee maker called Mr. Coffee. His friends must have smiled when they saw the ads. Still bothered by ulcers, Joe never drank coffee. Success as the Mr. Coffee spokesman brought more offers. Joe, always careful of his image, refused to sell beer or cigarettes. He did sign on with New York's Bowery Savings Bank. Over 20 years later, he was still making commercials for the bank.

TRIVIA 10

A Honus Wagner baseball card once sold for $415,000. What is the record price for a Joe DiMaggio baseball card?

To New Yorkers, it seemed as though Joe had never been away. As Toots Shor once said of his city, "It's Joe's town." But Joe's fame had spread beyond the Big Apple. In 1974, President Gerald Ford awarded him the Medal of Freedom. The medal honored his public service as well as his baseball feats. President Ford said that Joe was a fine role model for America's young people.

The years added lines to his face, but Joe seldom slowed down. Then, in 1987, his heart began to cause trouble. Surgeons implanted a pacemaker in his chest to regulate his heartbeat. As soon as he recovered, Joe went back to his busy schedule.

Joe DiMaggio (left) with the owner of the New York Yankees, George Steinbrenner

This photo of Joe was taken during batting practice for a 1935 game.

JOE DIMAGGIO, BASEBALL IMMORTAL

Visitors to baseball's Hall of Fame linger in front of Joe's bronze plaque. Four years after he retired, sportswriters elected him on the first ballot. The plaque's lettering pays tribute to his hitting streak, his home runs and his three MVP awards. But it cannot show the Yankee Clipper in action.

Ernie Sisto, a sports photographer, saw many of Joe's games. He recalls, "When he was out there in center field it was like a song; he had that graceful rhythm. A guy would hit a ball. He'd take a look at it and then he'd turn away and he'd run to a certain spot. . . . He knew where the ball was gonna go before the ball got there. He made it look so easy."

Second baseman Joe Gordon remembers Joe's clutch hitting. "I wish I had some records of the runs he drove in for us in games after the seventh, eighth and ninth innings," Gordon said. "The great players can do that."

Joe downplays this kind of talk. "I was six years old when I started playing baseball," he once told a writer. "I was good at it and I learned to handle the game. I handled the aches and pains and I handled the pressures. . . . I shied away from . . . the limelight. I just enjoyed playing the game."

The Yankee Clipper played his last major league game over 40 years ago. But fans both young and old line up to pay for his signature at autograph sessions. Joe picks up some easy bucks by signing baseball cards, scorecards and baseballs.

In 1987, Joe turned the tables during a dinner at the White House. President Ronald Reagan was playing host to Mikhail Gorbachev, the Soviet leader. Joe pulled out a baseball and asked Reagan if both men would sign it. "In my whole life," Joe said later, "that's the only time I ever asked anybody to sign a ball."

When the two leaders met the next day, Reagan pulled out the baseball. As Gorbachev signed, Reagan challenged the Russian to "play ball" on arms control. Four years later the talks started that day finally ended. Gorbachev and President George Bush signed a treaty that greatly reduced the threat of nuclear war.

Joe is shown in this 1935 game as he scores a run for the Yankees

That year—1991—was a big one for Joe. Sports pages and television features played up his 50-year-old hitting streak. Despite the excitement, Joe was his usual modest self. "I'm not one who likes to have all this attention," he said.

Will anyone ever break the record? Joe thinks it could happen. "Anybody who sprays the ball around has a chance," he says. "I just happened to be the one who went for the distance."

Baseball immortal Joe DiMaggio at age 17

GLOSSARY

amateur—Someone who competes for the love of sport, not for money.

batting average—A measure of a batter's success at the plate. Batting averages are figured by dividing the number of hits by the times at bat. Thus, someone who collects 35 hits in 100 at bats would have a batting average of .350.

draft—The process of calling up young men to serve in the armed forces during a time of national emergency.

dugout—The below-ground shelter where baseball players sit during a game when they're not playing.

Great Depression—The bad economic times that followed the stock market crash of 1929.

major leagues—The highest level of organized baseball. Only teams belonging to the American and National Leagues can be called major league.

old-timers game—An exhibition game played by retired major league stars.

pennant—A team that "wins a pennant" has won its league championship. Pennant winners go on to play in the World Series.

rookie—A ballplayer who is playing in the majors for the first time.

runs batted in (RBIs)—Players are given credit for an RBI when something they do as a batter enables a teammate to score.

sandlot game—A pickup baseball game played by children on a vacant lot or other open ground.

scout—Someone who checks out young ballplayers to see if they have what it takes to play professional baseball.

semipros—Ballplayers who are paid small amounts of money per game. Semipros usually play for teams sponsored by companies or small towns.

slump—A time during the season when everything seems to go wrong for a ballplayer. Batters who are in a slump cannot get their usual number of hits no matter how hard they try.

spring training—The weeks during which teams send their players to warm-weather states to prepare for the coming season.

MORE GOOD READING ABOUT JOE DIMAGGIO

Allen, Maury. *Where Have You Gone, Joe DiMaggio?* New York: E. P. Dutton & Co., 1975.

DeGregorio, George. *Joe DiMaggio: An Informal Biography.* New York: Stein and Day, 1981.

Halberstam, David. *Summer of '49.* New York: William Morrow and Co., 1989.

Kahn, Roger. *Joe & Marilyn: A Memory of Love.* New York: William Morrow and Co., 1986.

Seidel, Michael. *Streak: Joe DiMaggio and the Summer of '41.* New York: McGraw-Hill Book Co., 1988.

Silverman, Al. *Joe DiMaggio: The Golden Year 1941.* Englewood Cliffs, N.J.: Prentice-Hall, Inc., 1969.

Tullius, John. *"The Great DiMaggio." In I'd Rather Be a Yankee: An Oral History of America's Most Loved and Most Hated Baseball Team.* New York: Macmillan, 1986.

JOE DIMAGGIO TRIVIA QUIZ

1: As a nervous young rookie, Joe liked to relax by reading Superman comic books. When he listened to the radio, he enjoyed the quiz shows that were popular then.

2: Joe's managers did not turn him loose because they feared he would tear up his legs sliding into second. They wanted to keep his big bat in the lineup.

3: Strange as it may seem, Joe scored 56 runs and slashed 56 singles during his streak. His RBI total of 55 was only one short of that magic number.

4: During Joe's streak, the Yankees won 41 games and lost only 13 (two games ended in ties). Their winning percentage was a sparkling .759.

5: Williams won the batting crown that year by hitting a splendid .406. Joe's .357 was only third best in the American League.

6: Giuseppe DiMaggio gave all three boys the same middle name—Paul.

7: Joe ranked fifth on the list, ahead of Honus Wagner and Christy Mathewson. The top four, in order of their ranking, were Babe Ruth, Ty Cobb, Lou Gehrig and Walter Johnson.

8: Hank and Tommie Aaron hold the all-time home run record for brothers with 768. Hank hit 755 of them; Tommie hit 13.

9: Joe led the Yankees into the World Series in 10 of the 13 years he played for them. In 51 World Series games, he batted .249, with eight home runs and 30 RBIs. He appeared in 11 All-Star Games but never seemed to be at his best. Despite a lifetime batting average of .325, he hit only .225 in his 40 at bats in All-Star play.

10: In 1991, a Chicago collector paid $5,000 for a Joe DiMaggio Heads-Up Goudey card.

index